Gone Forever!

Ankylosaurus

Rupert Matthews

Heinemann Library
Chicago, Illinois

Customer Service 888-454-2279
Visit our website at www.heinemannlibrary.com

Produced for Heinemann Library by White-Thomson Publishing Ltd.
Edited by Kay Barnham
Book design by John Jamieson
Concept design by Ron Kamen and Paul Davies & Associates
Illustrations by James Field (SGA)
Originated by Que-Net Media™
Printed and bound in China by South China Printing Company

08 07 06 05
10 9 8 7 6 5 4 3 2

Library of Congress Cataloging-in-Publication Data
Matthews, Rupert.
Ankylosaurus / Rupert Matthews.
p. cm. -- (Gone forever!)
Summary: Discusses the ankylosaurus dinosaur, including its known physical characteristics, behavior, habitat, and what other creatures were contemporaneous with it, as well as how scientists study fossils and evaluate geological features to learn about extinct organisms.
Includes bibliographical references and index.
ISBN 1-4034-4909-0 (Hardcover) -- ISBN 1-4034-4916-3 (Paperback)
1. Ankylosaurus--Juvenile literature. [1. Ankylosaurus. 2. Dinosaurs.] I. Title.
QE862.O65M32 2004
567.915--dc22

2003016681

Acknowledgments
The author and publisher are grateful to the following for permission to reproduce copyright material:
Cover photograph reproduced with permission of the American Natural History Museum.
p. 4 GeoScience; p. 6 Pam E. Hickman/Natural Science Photos; p. 8 John Cancalosi/Okapia/OSF; pp. 10, 22, 24, 26 The Natural History Museum, London; p. 12 Corbis; p. 14 Camera Press; pp. 16, 18, 20 American Natural History Museum.

Special thanks to Dr. Peter Makovicky of the Chicago Field Museum for his review of this book.

Some words are shown in bold, **like this.** You can find out what they mean by looking in the glossary.

Contents

Gone Forever!

Some animals are **extinct.** This means that none remain alive anywhere in the world. Scientists find out about extinct animals by digging for **fossils** and then studying them.

One type of animal that became extinct was Ankylosaurus. This was a **dinosaur** that lived millions of years ago. Many other dinosaurs lived at the same time as Ankylosaurus. They are all now extinct.

Ankylosaurus' Home

Fossils of Ankylosaurus have been found in rocks in North America. Scientists called **geologists** study these rocks to find out what the area was like when Ankylosaurus lived there.

Ankylosaurus lived on high land, among hills and valleys. There were no forests, just bushes and a few trees. The weather was cool. At night it could become very cold on top of the hills.

Plants and Trees

leaf fossils

In the rocks near Ankylosaurus **fossils, geologists** have also found plant fossils. These plants grew when Ankylosaurus was alive. Some are now **extinct.** Others were like plants that grow today.

Before Ankylosaurus most plants were very green, like modern **fir** trees and **ferns.** When Ankylosaurus was alive, many plants appeared for the first time. These new plants had flowers and fruits.

Living with Ankylosaurus

Fossils of other animals have been found near those of Ankylosaurus. This means that they lived around the same time as Ankylosaurus. Most of these animals are now **extinct.**

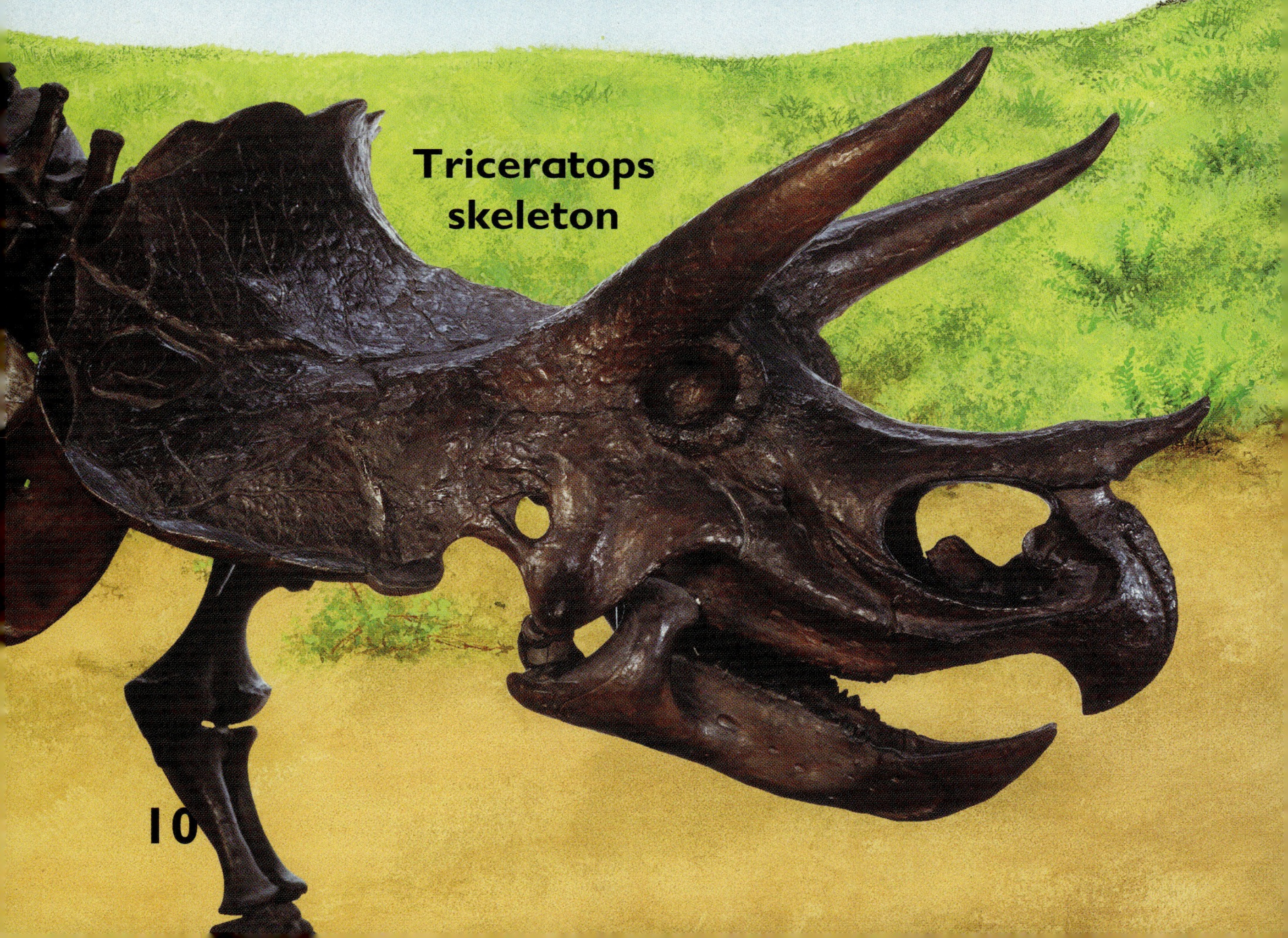

Triceratops skeleton

Triceratops lived on Earth when Ankylosaurus was alive. This was a type of **dinosaur** that ate plants. Triceratops lived in large **herds** that roamed on flat land and in valleys.

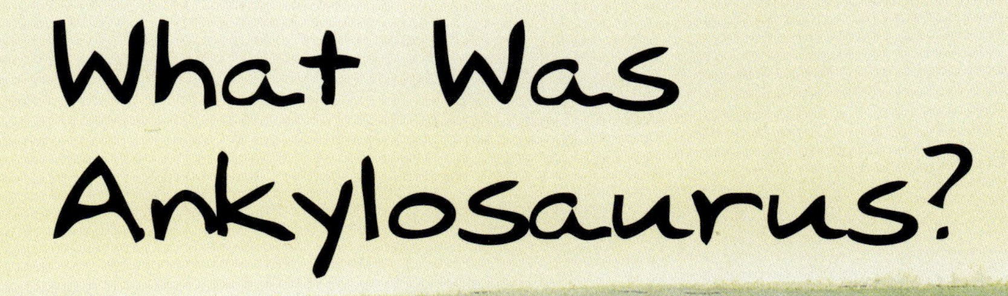

What Was Ankylosaurus?

Scientists called **paleontologists** examine **fossils** found in **ancient** rocks. By studying Ankylosaurus fossils, paleontologists have discovered what this **dinosaur** looked like.

Ankylosaurus model

Ankylosaurus was bigger than an elephant! It was covered in thick **armor** made of bone. It had a solid lump of bone on the end of its tail. Ankylosaurus' teeth show that it was a plant-eater.

Baby Ankylosaurus

Scientists have not yet found **fossils** of Ankylosaurus eggs. However, they have discovered fossils of very young Ankylosaurus, like the one below. These fossils show how baby Ankylosaurus lived.

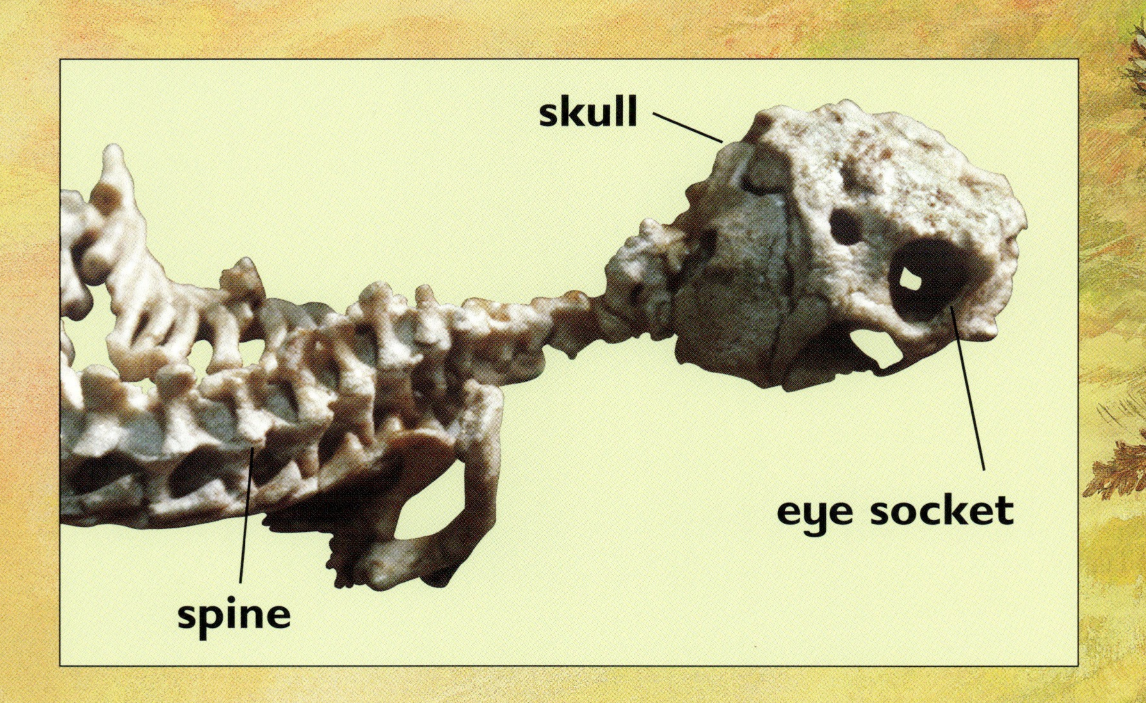

After they **hatched,** the baby Ankylosaurus stayed together. The young dinosaurs lived among bushes, safe from the meat-eating dinosaurs that wanted to eat them.

A Lonely Life

Scientists have found **fossils** of adult Ankylosaurus. However, they have never found groups of these **dinosaurs.** It seems that Ankylosaurus liked to live alone as it grew older.

Ankylosaurus skull

When the young Ankylosaurus had grown into an adult, it moved into hilly areas. Some scientists think that each Ankylosaurus had its own **territory,** which it guarded against other Ankylosaurus.

What Did Ankylosaurus Eat?

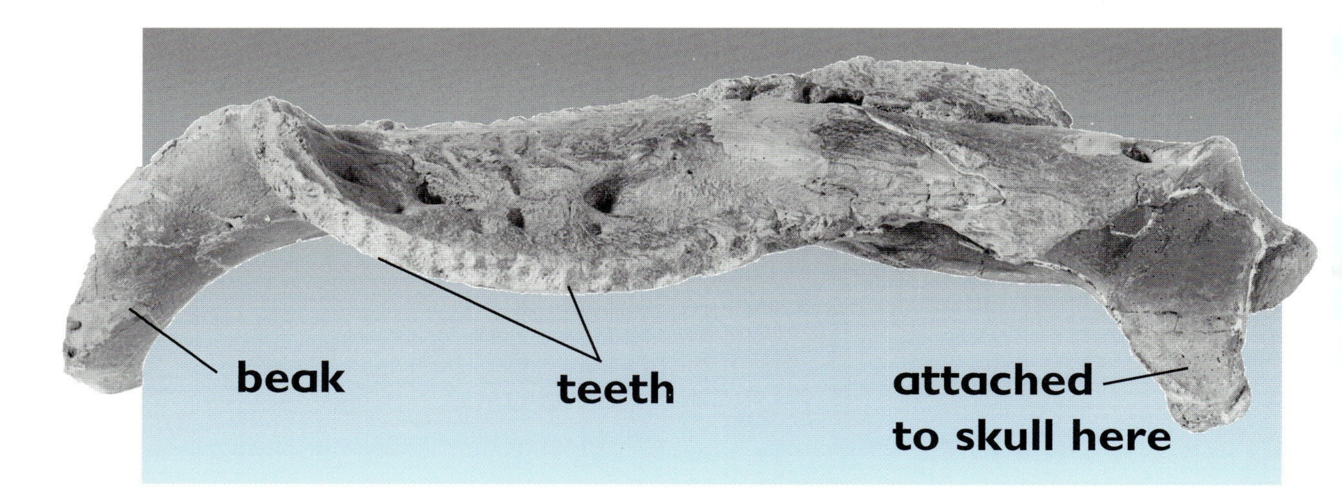

Ankylosaurus jawbone fossil

Ankylosaurus had small, weak teeth. This means that it probably ate soft foods. **Fossils** show that Ankylosaurus could not lift its head very high. Most of its food must have grown close to the ground.

Many scientists think Ankylosaurus ate fruit that grew on low bushes. These fruits were easy to reach. They were also soft and easy to chew. They would have made the perfect meal for Ankylosaurus.

Bone Armor

Ankylosaurus was **protected** by **armor** made of bone. The armor formed wide bands across Ankylosaurus' back. There were also round knobs of bone to protect weak areas.

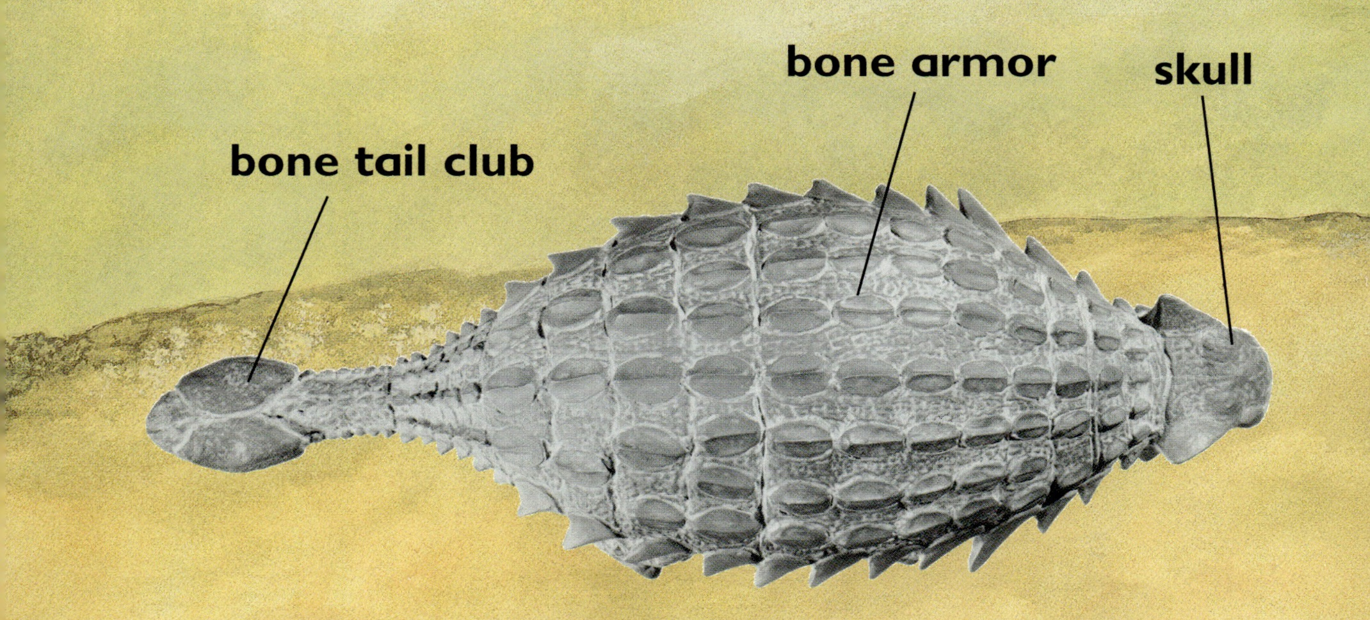

The bone armor covered most parts of Ankylosaurus. There were thick plates of bone on the top of the head and back of the neck. Even the eyelids were protected with armor.

The Club Tail

Ankylosaurus had a large lump of heavy bone on the end of its tail. Powerful **muscles** could swing the tail from side to side. Ankylosaurus may have used the lump of bone like a **club.**

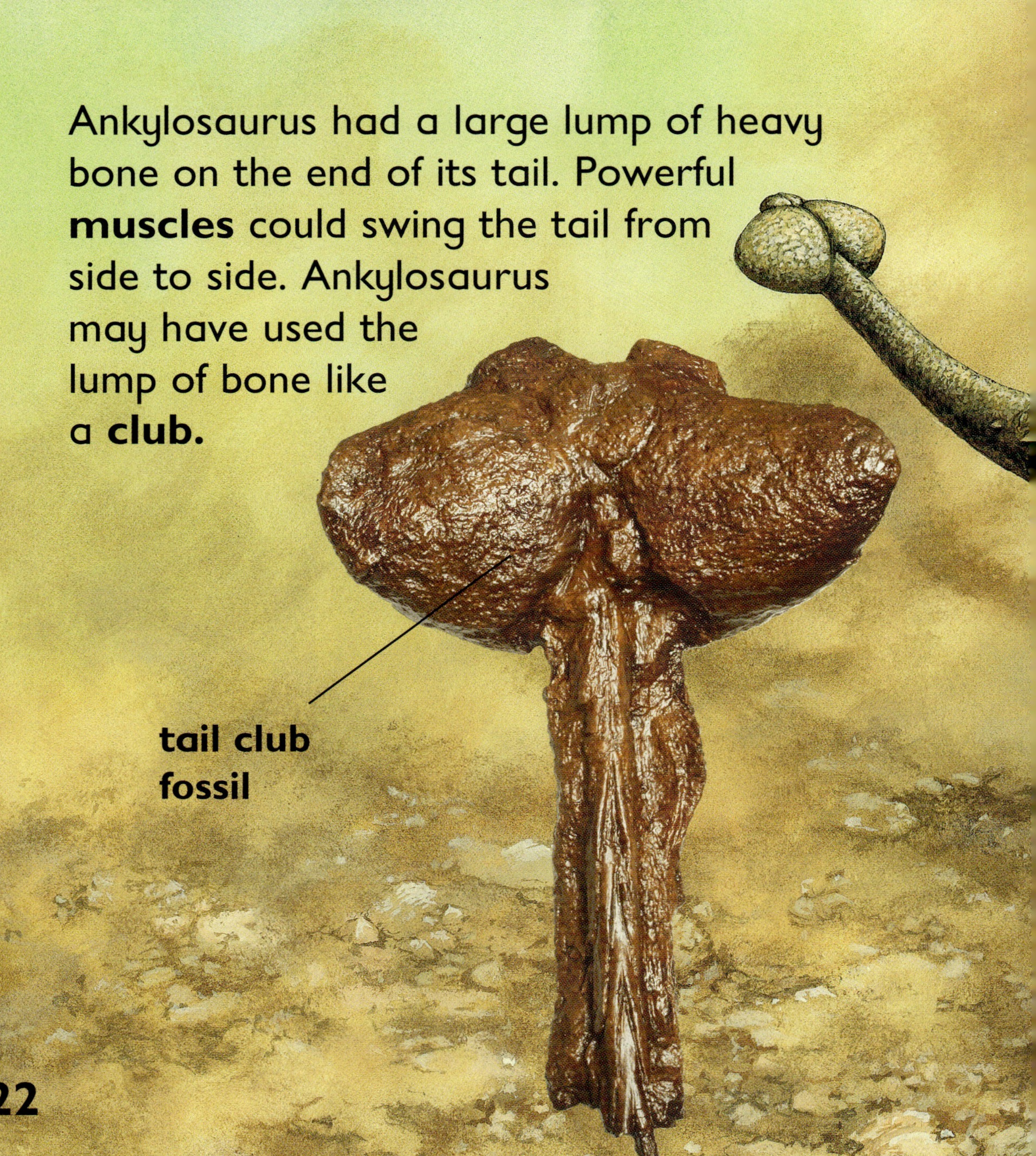

Two Ankylosaurus may have battled over food or **territories.** Some scientists think the **dinosaurs** may have pushed or hit each other with their tail clubs.

Under Attack!

close-up of Ankylosaurus armor

Tyrannosaurus was a meat-eating **dinosaur** that lived at the same time as Ankylosaurus. Tyrannosaurus was very powerful, with long, sharp teeth. It hunted and ate other dinosaurs.

Ankylosaurus may have used its **armor** to **protect** it from Tyrannosaurus. When it crouched down, only the armored parts of Ankylosaurus could be seen. It would have been difficult for Tyrannosaurus to attack.

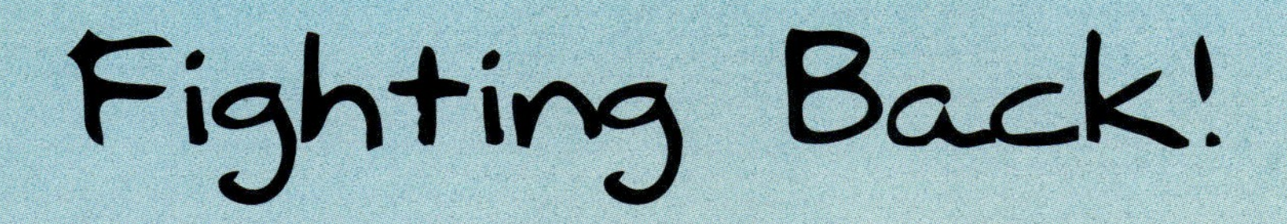

Fighting Back!

Ankylosaurus could have used its tail **club** to flight back against meat-eating **dinosaurs.** Even the **fierce** hunter **Tyrannosaurus** would have been stunned by a blow from the heavy tail club.

Tyrannosaurus skeleton

Ankylosaurus could have clubbed and injured an attacker and then escaped to safety.

Where Did Ankylosaurus Live?

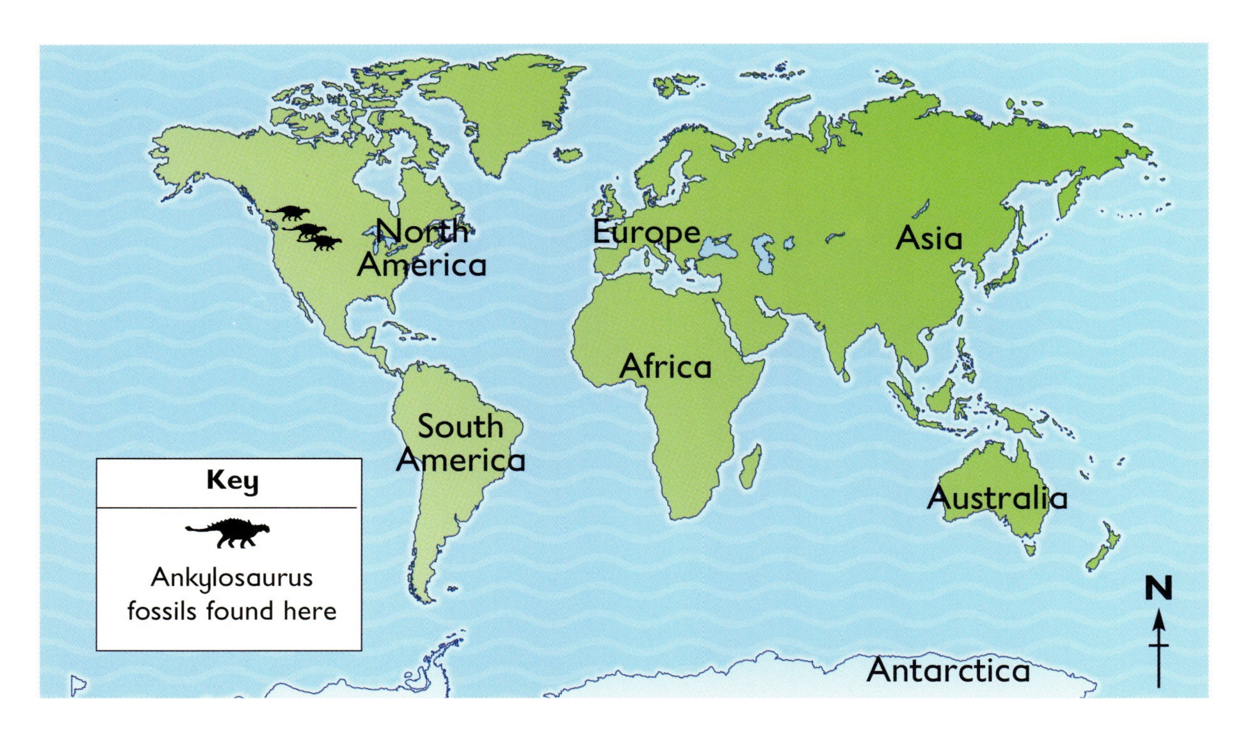

Ankylosaurus **fossils** have been found in the western half of North America. At the time of Ankylosaurus, this land was joined with Asia. The fossils of other **dinosaurs** like Ankylosaurus have also been found in Asia.

When Did Ankylosaurus Live?

Ankylosaurus lived between 65 and 61 million years ago. It lived at the end of the Mesozoic era, which is also known as the Age of the Dinosaurs. Ankylosaurus was one of the last dinosaurs to live on Earth.

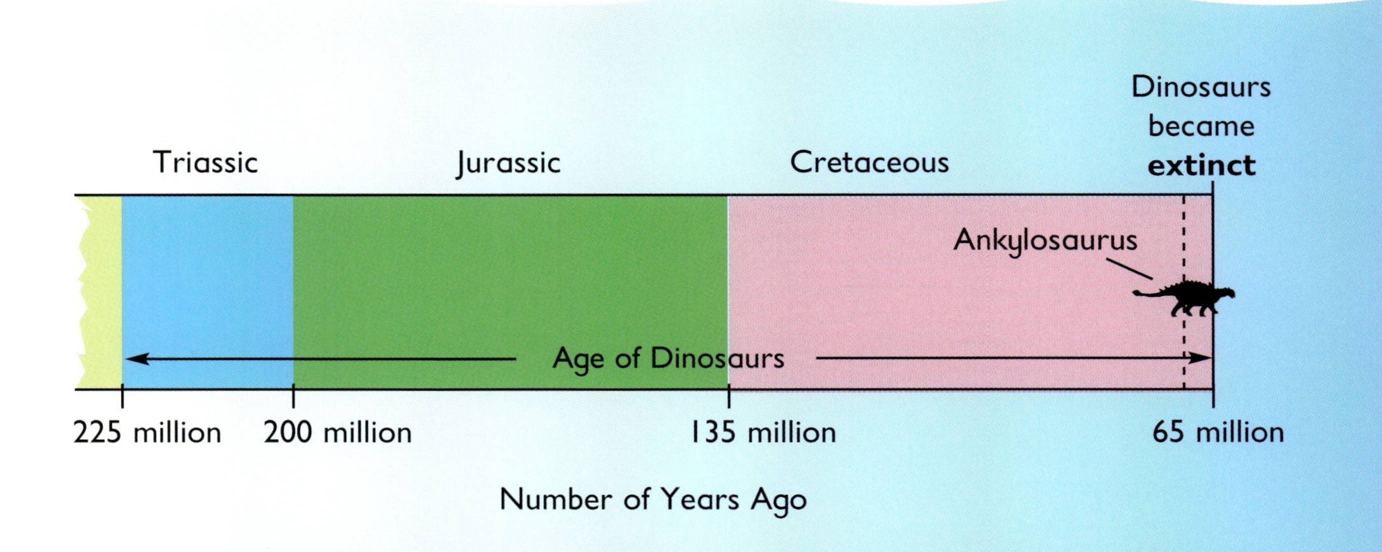

Fact File

Ankylosaurus	
Length:	about 30 feet (9 meters)
Height:	about 10 feet (3 meters)
Weight:	about 4 tons (4 metric tons)
Time:	late Cretaceous period, about 65 million years ago
Place:	western parts of North America

How to Say It

Ankylosaurus—ang-ky-lo-sawr-us
Cretaceous—kreh-tay-shus
dinosaur—dine-o-sawr
Jurassic—jer-as-ik
Mesozoic—meh-so-zo-ik
Pachycephalosaurus—pak-ee-kef-ah-lo-sawr-us
paleontologist—pay-lee-on-tah-lo-jist
Parasaurolophus—para-sawr-o-lo-fus
Quetzalcoatlus—kayt-zal-ko-at-lus
Thescelosaurus—thes-keh-lo-sawr-us
Triassic—try-as-ik
Triceratops—try-ser-ah-tops
Tyrannosaurus—ty-ran-o-sawr-us

Glossary

ancient very old
armor protective covering of hard material
club stick with a lump on one end that is used as a weapon
dinosaur reptile that lived on Earth between 228 and 65 million years ago but has died out
extinct once lived on Earth but has died out
fern green plant with large feathery leaves and no flowers
fierce showing violent, wild energy
fir tree with flat, needle-shaped leaves that stay green all year
fossil remains of a plant or animal, usually found in rocks
geologist scientist who studies rocks
hatch break out of an egg
herd group of animals that live together
muscle part of an animal's body that makes it move
Pachycephalosaurus large plant-eating dinosaur with a domed head
paleontologist scientist who studies the fossils of animals or plants that have died out
Parasaurolophus large plant-eating dinosaur with a beak
protect keep safe from danger
Quetzalcoatlus type of pterosaur, or flying reptile
territory piece of land where an animal lives
Thescelosaurus plant-eating dinosaur that could run quickly
Triceratops type of dinosaur with three horns on its head
Tyrannosaurus type of dinosaur that hunted other dinosaurs

More Books to Read

Cohen, Daniel. *Ankylosaurus.* Mankato, Minn.: Capstone, 2003.

Dahl, Michael. *Dinosaur World.* Minneapolis, Minn.: Picture Window Books, 2003.

Goecke, Michael P. *Ankylosaurus.* Edina, Minn.: ABDO, 2002.

Matthews, Rupert. *Triceratops.* Chicago, Ill.: Heinemann Library, 2003.

Index